D0270262

DINOSAUR JUNIORS
Wide Awake

this book belongs to

....
.   .
.   .
....

9 22000001 22 490

Once
a
long
upon
long
long
long
long
long
For the human
Otto and Winnie.
And Alice.
long
long
long
long
long

DINOSAUR JUNIORS
Wide Awake

Written and illustrated by

Rob Biddulph

HarperCollins *Children's Books*

First published in hardback in Great Britain by
HarperCollins Children's Books in 2019
This paperback edition first published in 2019

HarperCollins Children's Books is a division of HarperCollins Publishers Ltd.
Text and illustrations copyright © Rob Biddulph 2019
The author / illustrator asserts the moral right to be identified as the
author / illustrator of the work. A CIP catalogue record for this book
is available from the British Library. All rights reserved.

No part of this publication may be reproduced, stored in a retrieval system,
or transmitted in any form or by any means, electronic, mechanical,
photocopying, recording or otherwise, without the prior permission of
HarperCollins Publishers Ltd, 1 London Bridge Street, London SE1 9GF.

Visit our website at www.harpercollins.co.uk

ISBN: 978-0-00-831801-7
Printed and bound in China
10 9 8 7 6 5 4 3 2 1

FIVE THINGS TO FIND IN THIS BOOK
1. A ringing alarm clock ▪
2. A prehistoric bat ▪
3. A box of Dino Krispies ▪
4. A dandelion ▪
5. A visitor from outer space ▪

long long long long long long long long long long

time ago...

The light fades with the setting sun.
This dino-twosome's day is done.

Nice, clean faces...

Sparkling teeth...

And cosy quilts to lie beneath.

"Once upon a moonlit night..."

Dino Snores
A bedtime story collection

A kiss from Mum.
"Sweet dreams.
Sleep tight."

The brightest stars.

The stillest lake.

But somebody
is wide awake.

"Hey?" says Winnie.

Not a peep.

Then...

A dozy Otto lifts his head.
And slowly sits up in his bed.

"Right,"
he says,
"this won't
take long.
We simply
need a
sleepy song.

Settle down,
and I will try
To sing
a soothing
lullaby."

"Twinkle twinkle meteor,

Glowing like a firefly.

Twinkle twinkle meteor,

High above this dinosaur.

Blaze a trail across the sky.

High above this dinosaur."

Well done, Otto.
Piece of cake.

But wait...

Oh dear. She's still awake.

A sleepy Otto sips his drink.
He yawns and has another think...

"Ok, Winnie.
How about
A memory game
to tire you out?

List all the things
we did today,
Then close your
eyes and drift
away..."

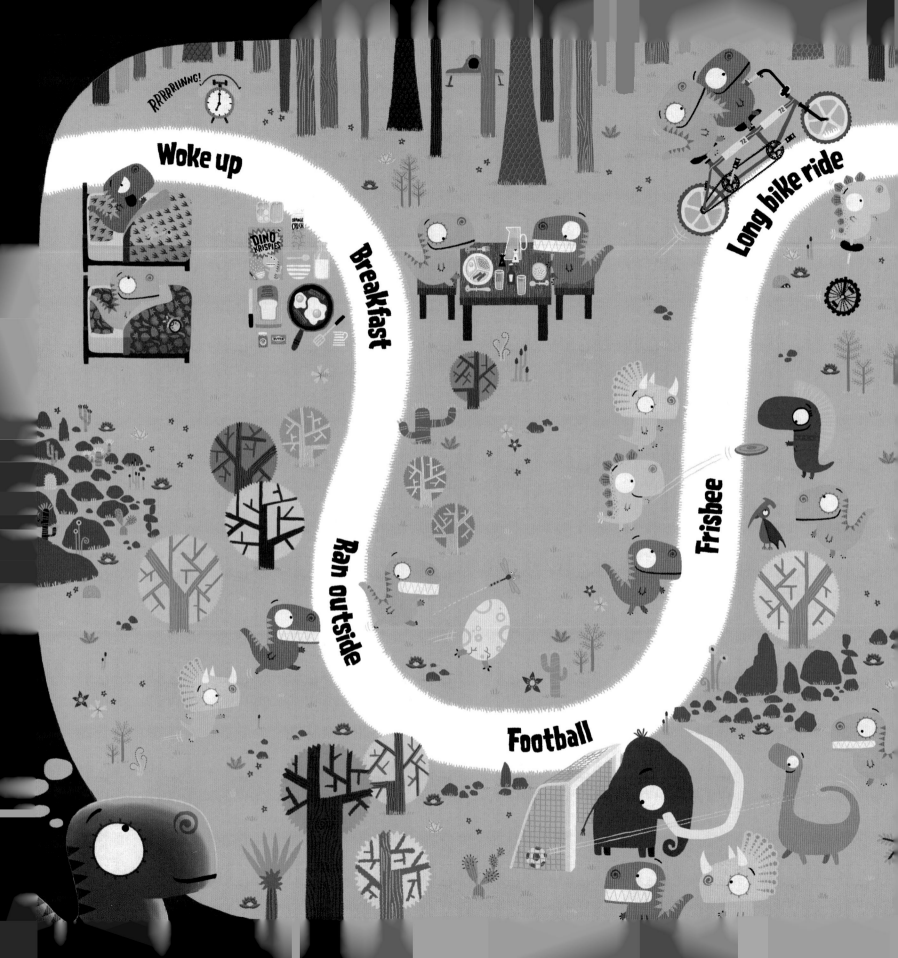

Woke up

Breakfast

Long bike ride

Ran outside

Frisbee

Football

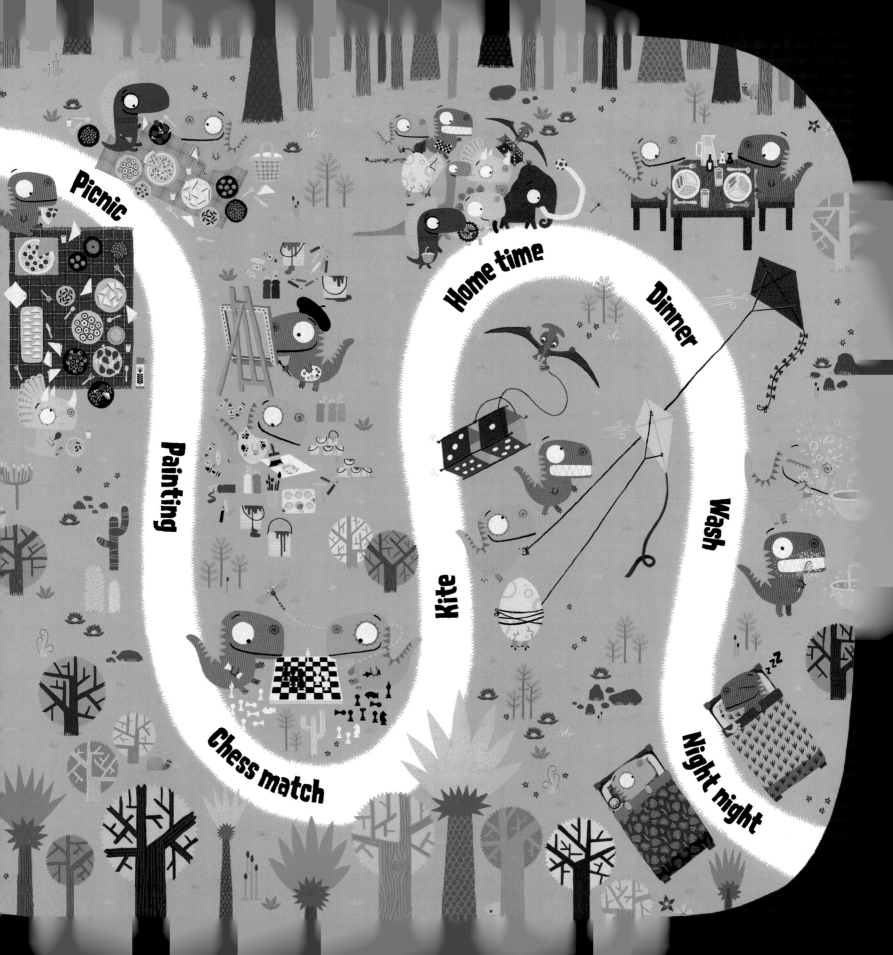

Picnic

Painting

Chess match

Kite

Home time

Dinner

Wash

Night night

Nice work, Otto.
Big handshake.

But wait...

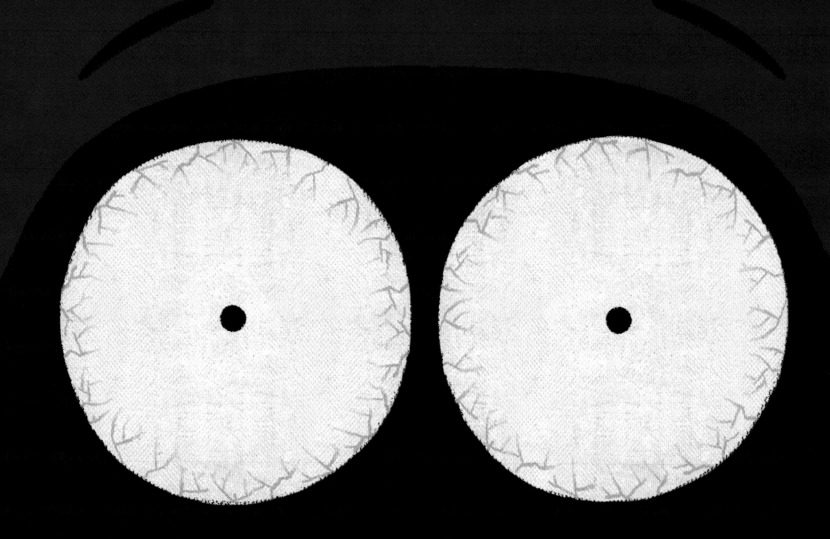

No way! She's still awake!

A weary Otto sighs a sigh.
"Right," he says, "just one more try."

"Picture this to fall asleep:
A field, a fence, some dino-sheep.

Now close your eyes and concentrate
And count how many jump the gate."

Counting sheep is won der ful !

(Can you try to count them too? You might just doze off if you do...)

Great job, Otto!
Major win!

And look! At last!
A sleeping twin!

So ends another busy day.
With moon and stars to light our way
Through golden slumbers, long and deep.

Then...

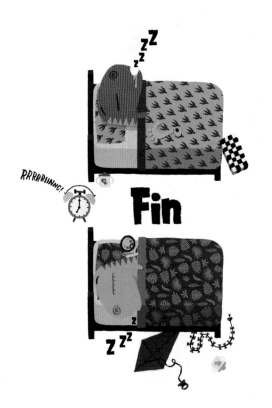